For Robert

First published 1994 by Walker Books Ltd
87 Vauxhall Walk, London SE11 5HJ

This edition published 2003

4 6 8 10 9 7 5

© 1994 Nick Sharratt

The right of Nick Sharratt to be identified as author/illustrator
respectively of this work has been asserted by him in accordance
with the Copyright, Designs and Patents Act 1988

This book has been typeset in Arial

Printed in China

British Library Cataloguing in Publication Data:
a catalogue record for this book is available from the British Library

ISBN: 978-0-7445-9499-7

My Mum and Dad
make me laugh

Nick Sharratt

WALKER BOOKS
AND SUBSIDIARIES

LONDON · BOSTON · SYDNEY · AUCKLAND

My mum and dad make me laugh.

One likes spots and the other likes stripes.

My mum likes spots in winter

and spots in summer.

My dad likes stripes on weekdays

and stripes at weekends.

Last weekend we went to the safari park. My mum put on her spottiest dress and earrings, and my dad put on his stripiest suit and tie.

I put on my grey top and trousers.
"You do like funny clothes!" said my mum and dad.

We set off in the car and on the way we stopped for something to eat.
My mum had a spotty pizza and my dad had a stripy ice cream.

I had a bun. "You do like funny food!" said my mum and dad.

When we got to the safari park it was very exciting.
My mum liked the big cats best.

"Those are splendid spots," she said. "And I should know!"

My dad liked the zebras best.

"Those are super stripes," he said. "And I should know!"

But the animals I liked best didn't have spots and didn't have stripes.
They were big and grey and eating their tea.

"Those are really good elephants," I said.

"And I should know!"

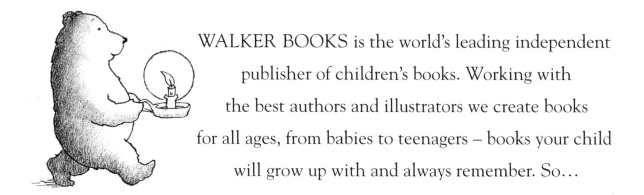

WALKER BOOKS is the world's leading independent publisher of children's books. Working with the best authors and illustrators we create books for all ages, from babies to teenagers – books your child will grow up with and always remember. So…

FOR THE BEST CHILDREN'S BOOKS, LOOK FOR THE BEAR